He lived in a house on a hill which he'd built himself.

A not very clever house!

One of Mr Dizzy's problems was that he lived in a country where everybody else was terribly clever.

Cleverland!

Even the birds were clever in Cleverland!

Everything and everybody in Cleverland was clever.

You'll never see a worm reading a book anywhere else but Cleverland.

Poor Mr Dizzy. Everything around him was so clever it made his head spin.

One morning Mr Dizzy was out for a walk when he met a pig.

"What's big and grey and has big ears and a trunk?" said the clever pig to Mr Dizzy.

"Er! A mouse?" said Mr Dizzy.

The pig laughed sarcastically at Mr Dizzy, and went off shaking his head.

Then Mr Dizzy met an elephant.

A clever elephant.

"What's small and furry and likes cheese?" the elephant asked cleverly.

"Er. A pig?" replied Mr Dizzy.

The clever elephant laughed down his trunk. "A pig?" he trumpeted. "A pig? You silly man!" And off he went.

Poor Mr Dizzy!

Mr Dizzy decided he didn't want to talk to anybody else that day, so he went for a walk in the wood, where he knew that he wouldn't meet anybody.

He felt very miserable about not being clever, and as he walked along a tear trickled down his cheek.

Poor Mr Dizzy.

Then, in the middle of the wood, he came across a well.

Little did Mr Dizzy know that it was a wishing well.

The day was warm, and so he decided to take a drink of water from the well.

Mr Dizzy drank deeply.

But, he was still unhappy.

"Oh, I wish I could be clever," he sighed.

Little did Mr Dizzy know that, whoever drinks deeply from the water at the wishing well, his wish will come true.

And Mr Dizzy had wished that he could be clever.

And his wish had come true.

He was clever.

But he didn't know it.

Not yet!

On the way home, Mr Dizzy came across the elephant and the pig he had met earlier.

They were telling each other about how they had made Mr Dizzy look silly by asking him a question he couldn't answer.

They were giggling and sniggering about it, when they saw Mr Dizzy approaching from the wood.

"Here he comes again," giggled the clever pig.

"Let's ask him another question," sniggered the clever elephant.

Mr Dizzy came up to them.

"Tell us," said the clever pig, trying to keep a straight face. "What's white and woolly and goes Baaa?"

"Why, a sheep of course," replied Mr Dizzy.

The pig and the elephant were amazed.

To tell the truth, so too was Mr Dizzy.

He suddenly felt very very clever.

It was a not unpleasant feeling.

"Tell us," said the clever elephant. "What has four legs, a tail and goes Woof?"

"How easy," replied Mr Dizzy. "A dog of course!"

The clever pig and the clever elephant couldn't understand how Mr Dizzy had become so clever in one morning.

Mr Dizzy couldn't understand how he had become so clever in one morning.

But we know how he'd become so clever in one morning.

Don't we?

"Now, let me ask you a question," said Mr Dizzy to the pig.

"You?" grunted the pig rudely. "You ask me a question? Don't be ridiculous! There's no question you could ask me that I couldn't answer!"

"Really?" smiled Mr Dizzy. "Well then, can you tell me what's fat and pink and goes Atishoo, Atishoo?"

"What's fat and pink and goes Atishoo, Atishoo?" repeated the pig looking worried. "There's nothing that's fat and pink and goes Atishoo, Atishoo!"

"Nothing, eh?" said Mr Dizzy, and he tickled the pig's nose.

"Atishoo, Atishoo," sneezed the pig.

"The answer is you," said Mr Dizzy. "You're fat and pink and you're going Atishoo, Atishoo!"

The clever pig looked downright, if not downleft, miserable.

Mr Dizzy turned to the elephant.

Who, incidentally, had stopped sniggering.

"Now," said Mr Dizzy. "Let me ask you a question. What's large and grey and goes Dopit, Dopit?"

"What's large and grey and goes Dopit, Dopit?" repeated the elephant looking worried. "There's nothing that's large and grey and goes Dopit, Dopit."

"Oh yes there is," grinned Mr Dizzy. "There certainly is something that's large and grey and goes Dopit, Dopit," and he tied a knot in the clever elephant's trunk.

"Dop it! Dop it!" cried the elephant, who wanted to say, "Stop it! Stop it!" but couldn't talk properly with a knot in his trunk.

Mr Dizzy grinned, and went home.

"I duppose doo dink dat's fuddy," said the elephant.

3 Great Offers For Mr Men Fans

1 Token · EGMONT WORLD

1 FREE Door Hangers and Posters

In every Mr Men and Little Miss Book like this one you will find a special token. Collect 6 and we will send you either a brilliant Mr. Men or Little Miss poster and a Mr Men or Little Miss double sided, full colour, bedroom door hanger. Apply using the coupon overleaf, enclosing six tokens and a 50p coin for your choice of two items.

Egmont World tokens can be used towards any other Egmont World / World International token scheme promotions, in early learning and story / activity books.

Posters: Tick your preferred choice of either Mr Men ☐ or Little Miss ☐

Door Hangers: Choose from: Mr. Nosey & Mr Muddle ☐, Mr Greedy & Mr Lazy ☐, Mr Tickle & Mr Grumpy ☐, Mr Slow & Mr Busy ☐ Mr Messy & Mr Quiet ☐, Mr Perfect & Mr Forgetful ☐, Little Miss Fun & Little Miss Late ☐, Little Miss Helpful & Little Miss Tidy ☐, Little Miss Busy & Little Miss Brainy ☐, Little Miss Star & Little Miss Fun ☐. (Please tick)

2 Mr Men Library Boxes

Keep your growing collection of Mr Men and Little Miss books in these superb library boxes. With an integral carrying handle and stay-closed fastener, these full colour, plastic boxes are fantastic. They are just £5.49 each including postage. Order overleaf.

3 Join The Club

To join the fantastic Mr Men & Little Miss Club, check out the page overleaf NOW!

Join Our Club!

MR MEN & Little Miss CLUB

When you become a member of the fantastic Mr Men and Little Miss Club you'll receive a personal letter from Mr Happy and Little Miss Giggles, a club badge with your name, and a superb Welcome Pack (pictured below right).

You'll also get birthday and Christmas cards from the Mr Men and Little Misses, 2 newsletters crammed with special offers, privileges and news, and a copy of the 12 page Mr Men catalogue which includes great party ideas.

If it were on sale in the shops, the Welcome Pack alone might cost around £13. But a year's membership is just £9.99 (plus 73p postage) with a 14 day money-back guarantee if you are not delighted!

HOW TO APPLY To apply for any of these three great offers, ask an adult to complete the coupon below and send it with appropriate payment and tokens (where required) to: Mr Men Offers, PO Box 7, Manchester M19 2HD. Credit card orders for Club membership ONLY by telephone, please call: 01403 242727.

To be completed by an adult

❑ **1.** Please send a poster and door hanger as selected overleaf. I enclose six tokens and a 50p coin for post (coin not required if you are also taking up 2. or 3. below).

❑ **2.** Please send __ Mr Men Library case(s) and __ Little Miss Library case(s) at £5.49 each.

❑ **3.** Please enrol the following in the Mr Men & Little Miss Club at £10.72 (inc postage)

Fan's Name:_____Fan's Address:_____

_____Post Code:_____Date of birth:___ /___ /___

Your Name:_____Your Address:_____

_____

Post Code:_____Name of parent or guardian (if not you):_____

Total amount due: £_____ (£5.49 per Library Case, £10.72 per Club membership)

❑ I enclose a cheque or postal order payable to Egmont World Limited.

❑ Please charge my MasterCard / Visa account.

Card number: | | | | | | | | | | | | | | | | |

Expiry Date: _____/_____   Signature: _____

Data Protection Act: If you do **not** wish to receive other family offers from us or companies we recommend, please tick this box ❑. Offer applies to UK only